Night of the
White Deer

By Jack Bushnell   Illustrated by Miguel Co

Tanglewood • Terre Haute, IN

For my father and mother,
who taught me to follow the white deer.
-JB

Published by Tanglewood Publishing, Inc., October, 2012
Text © 2012 Jack Bushnell
Illustrations © 2012 Miguel Co

Design by Amy Alick Perich

Tanglewood Publishing, Inc.
4400 Hulman St.
Terre Haute, IN 47803
www.tanglewoodbooks.com

Printed in China
10 9 8 7 6 5 4 3 2 1

ISBN 1-933718-80-3
ISBN 978-1-933718-80-4

Library of Congress Cataloging-in-Publication Data

Bushnell, Jack.
 Night of the white deer / Jack Bushnell ; Miguel Co.
    p. cm.
 Summary: Having heard stories all his life about a strange white deer, a boy sees a glowing, albino doe and follows her on a magical journey through the Northern Lights.
  ISBN 978-1-933718-80-4 (hardback) -- ISBN 1-933718-80-3
 [1. Supernatural--Fiction. 2. Deer--Fiction. 3. Auroras--Fiction. 4. Farm life--Fiction.] I. Co, Miguel, ill. II. Title.
 PZ7.B96547Nig 2012
 [Fic]--dc23
                       2012010149

The white deer walked into our cornfield
last night. She stood under the moon and
glowed like a fallen star.

Some folks say that's just what she is. A star that fell to earth and took the shape of the first thing it saw.

Others tell stories of the year the tornado hit the Olson farm. It wrecked their dairy barn and smashed their milk tanks. But they say the milk didn't soak into the ground; it rose up and formed itself into a creamy white, long-legged doe. Then it raced the tornado over the hill. And it won.

I couldn't figure out what my dad thought about the white deer. Mostly, when my brother and I brought it up, he'd tell us to go do our chores or something. And that would put an end to our talk. But now and then, he seemed to listen real hard, like he hoped we'd say more.

I mentioned this to my brother once. He laughed. "What do *you* know? You're a little kid. The white deer is make-believe." He rolled his eyes. "Haven't you figured that out yet?"

So when I saw the albino
deer last night, I wasn't sure
what to think, but I knew what
to do. I crawled out of my
bedroom window, climbed down
the rainspout, and went to her.

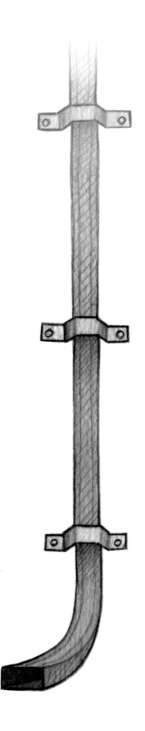

Together we walked between the rows of corn. I was close enough to touch her, but I didn't. Her coat sparkled like sunlight on water. I felt her heat in the summer air.

When we'd walked awhile and I could no longer see my house and our barn, the white deer stopped. We'd left the cornfields and now stood deep in alfalfa.

"Why are we here?" I asked.

The deer looked up. I did, too.

High above us, where there had been only darkness, the air now burned with colors. Oranges and reds and shimmering greens, and blinding white specks that fell like snow toward the earth.

The sky rolled like a glittering ocean against a black shore.

The more I stared up, the less I felt the
ground beneath my feet. I raised my hands to
all the colors and felt them pull me toward them.
The air around me popped and flashed. It crackled
and buzzed. My skin tingled, and my heart felt
big enough to hold the whole sky.

Far below, my house stood quietly in the
valley, washed gray by the moon. The barn, the
silo, and the corncrib looked as they always had.
But up here, the air glistened like paints
thrown over a black canvas.

The deer had bounded into the
lights. She was not alone. Countless
other creatures seemed to live within
the blazing colors:

Red gazelles, leaping and prancing
across the sky.

Mighty black elk, their antlers
sizzling as they tossed their heads and
crashed against one another.

Antelope, striped with light, splashing in
luminous green waters.

And thousands of white deer. Maybe millions. Racing before the stars, first one direction, then another. I could no longer see the deer that had brought me.

I whirled and turned and danced the dance of the aurora, while all around me the creatures of the sky danced, too.

Up, up we went until we burst from the sea of
light into the cool, deep darkness of space. The
earth curved below me, a bright blue ball. And
over its surface, ribbons of fire.

I thought that I would never stop, that I
would go higher and higher until I reached Mars
and crossed the rings of Saturn.

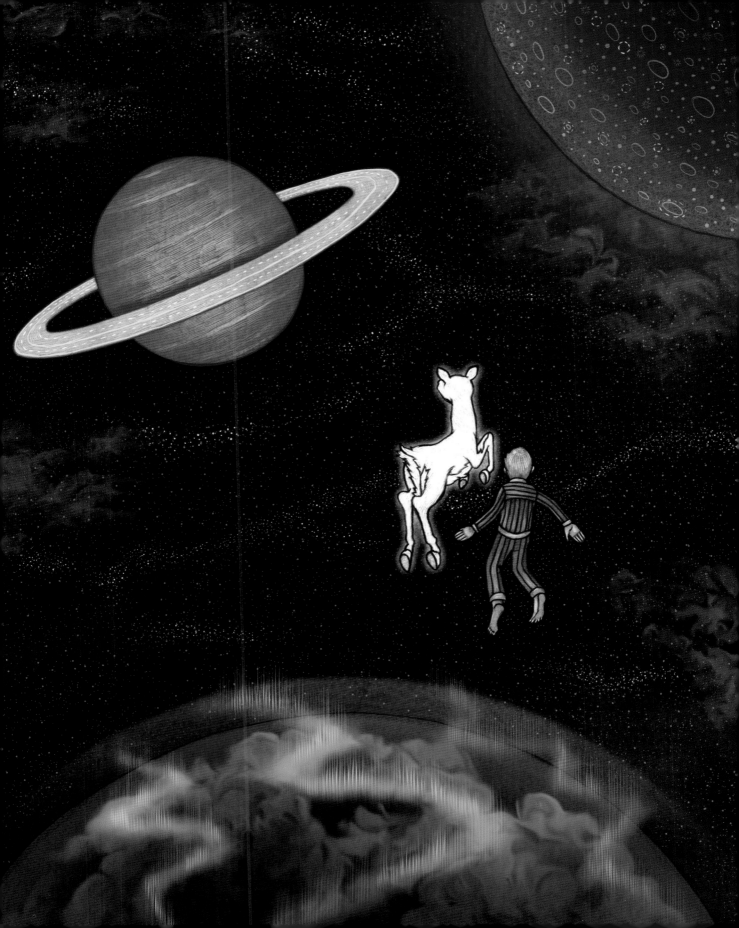

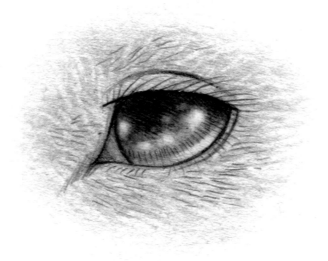

But my white deer came to fetch me. She led me home. Back down into the lights. Through the swarms of antelope, elk, and gazelle. Through the fields of alfalfa and corn and into my own backyard.

There she left me, but not before I'd reached out and touched the fur of her neck, whiter than rippling snow.

The next thing I knew, I was squinting into the morning sun. I'd slept the rest of the night sitting by my bedroom window. The deer was gone.

"A lot of folks think somebody made up that albino deer story," my mom said at breakfast after I'd told everyone what had happened. "But who knows?" She winked at me over the top of her coffee cup.

Dad leaned against the kitchen counter. He watched me and said nothing.

My brother snickered. "You dreamed it," he said. "There's no white deer. Right, Dad?"

Mom stood up. "Why don't we check on those piglets?" she said. She left the house, my brother close behind her.

I was about to follow, but Dad stopped me. "What did she look like?" he asked.

"All white," I said. "Whiter than milk. Whiter than ice cream." I looked down at my boots. "Maybe I dreamed her."

"No," he said. I looked up at him in surprise. "You didn't dream her. She came to me, too, when I was your age. She took me to see the Northern Lights." For a moment his face looked sad. Then he grinned. "I've waited a long time for her to return."

Dad laid his hand on my shoulder. Suddenly I
felt just a little taller, as if I'd grown since yesterday.
I can't explain it, but the feeling made me smile.

"Tell you what," said Dad. "If the white deer
comes again, will you wake me and take me
with you?"

"Sure," I told him.

"Good." He gave a little laugh. "Thanks."

Dad handed me my cap, and together we
walked out to do our chores.